Spike

Roary

Clawdie

For Ethan
-P.H.

For Eva,
Love Dad x
-D.G.

tiger tales

5 River Road, Suite 128, Wilton, CT 06897
Published in the United States 2022
Text by Patricia Hegarty
Text copyright © 2022 Caterpillar Books Ltd.
Illustrations copyright © 2022 Dean Gray
ISBN-13: 978-1-68010-290-1
ISBN-10: 1-68010-290-7
Printed in China • CPB/2800/2054/1221
2 4 6 8 10 9 7 5 3 1

www.tigertalesbooks.com

The TINYSAURS
Trick-or-Treat

by
Patricia Hegarty

tiger tales

Illustrated by
Dean Gray

It's that spooky time of year again,
when ghosts and witches are seen.
There is dressing up to trick-or-treat —
the Tinysaurs LOVE Halloween!

As they race to get the house ready,
there is a lot of work to be done.
Roary gets wrapped up in cobwebs...

There's excitement
when the doorbell rings;
Roary runs to
see who is there.

Clawdie goes to
find some candy,
but — oh-no!
— the cupboard is bare!

The disappointed trick-or-treaters
are a very sorry sight.
Sad skeletons and somber spiders
head off slowly into the night.

The Tinysaurs have a big problem:
They have no treats to give away.

They need a plan — and quickly —
before they ruin everyone's day!

Suddenly, Clawdie has an idea:
"*I* know what we should do!
It's the only way to get some treats —
we'll go trick-or-treating, too!"

With the help of some
sticky bandages,

a pumpkin, and
a sheet,

the Tinysaurs get
busy with costumes....

Their transformation is now complete!

Clawdie looks just like a mummy,
and Spike makes an awesome ghost.
But Roary's pumpkin costume
is the one they love the most!

As they set off on their adventure,
the Tinysaurs look the part.
A mummy, a ghost, and a pumpkin —
let the trick-or-treating start!

KEEP

OUT

KNOCK
KNOCK!

The Tinysaurs knock on their first front door,
and Roary cries, "Trick or treat!"

They are met with smiles and laughter
and are rewarded with something sweet.

As they make their way from house to house,
Spike and Roary are having fun.
But Clawdie is having a problem —
her bandages are coming undone!

As poor Clawdie
slowly unravels,

Spike is falling to pieces, too.
His spikes are poking
through the sheet.
He doesn't know what to do!

Roary is such a cute pumpkin
that he found a new furry friend

who seems to think he's a chew toy —
will this night never end?

The Tinysaurs ring the next doorbell
and are met with a chorus of screams.
This is the best reaction yet —
they didn't need any costumes, it seems!

ROAR!

They return to Tinysaur Mansion
with plenty of treats to share.
Everyone is invited in —
there are monsters everywhere!

"Clawdie! Let's put on some music!"
calls Spike as he takes to the floor.
Halloween just wouldn't be Halloween
without a dancing dinosaur!

The party is over, the dancing is done,
and it's finally time to rest.
The Tinysaurs have all agreed —
Halloween is simply the best!